The Twins and the Wild Ghost Chase

Paul Mason

Illustrated by Mike Phillips

BLOOMSBURY EDUCATION

For Jenny
How do I even begin…

First published 2016 by Bloomsbury Education
an imprint of Bloomsbury Publishing Plc
50 Bedford Square
London WC1B 3DP

www.bloomsbury.com

Bloomsbury is a registered trademark of Bloomsbury Publishing Plc

ISBN: 978-1-4729-1654-9

A CIP catalogue for this book is available from the British Library.

Printed and bound by CPI Group (UK) Ltd, Croydon CR0 4YY

1 3 5 7 9 10 8 6 4 2

Contents

Principal players		1
Prologue		2
Chapter One	Holograms	5
Chapter Two	Homesick	11
Chapter Three	"The game's afoot"	17
Chapter Four	"All present and accounted for"	24
Chapter Five	One down	30
Chapter Six	"O Romeo, Romeo! Wherefore art thou Romeo?"	39
Chapter Seven	Gibber, jabber	46
Chapter Eight	One-nil to the Fusiliers	55
Chapter Nine	Number One, London	62
Chapter Ten	A battle lost	68
Chapter Eleven	Another wild ghost chase	76
Chapter Twelve	Duncan MacAngus, poet	85
Chapter Thirteen	Waterloo	91

Principal players

Stella and Tom: twins

Harry Parkin: Stella and Tom's guardian and castle caretaker

Seymour Stoneyheart: ghost-catcher

Field Marshal Arthur Wellesley, 1st Duke of Wellington, KG GCB GCH PC FRS (1769-1852)

Reg Butcher: centre forward, Fusiliers F.C. (1897-1966)

Gelatina: belly dancer, actor (1923-1968)

Headmaster Staines: headmaster, Strapping Manor Grammar School (1875-1955)

Marcus Severus Occulus: Roman legionary (AD 43-68)

Prologue

It was a gentle day towards the end of July, the sort where a soft haze drifts across the English Channel like silk and everything seems still and lazy, making you wish you'd remembered your swimming togs and had a tall glass of cold lemonade.

As it was the holidays, the grand castle facing out to sea was open for business, and life murmured within its thick, stone walls just as it had done for hundreds of years. (Except of course, for those times when Henry VIII used to drop in, and there was less of a murmuring and more of a thundering and a bellowing.)

Today, things were ticking along nicely. In the gift shop, pots of golden honey and cloth dolls found homes in paper bags. Entry tickets changed hands, books were thumbed, rubber swords swished, and a pretty postcard chosen for Aunt Cecily (even though she didn't really deserve it – the mean, old walrus). In the café, muffins were flying out like hot cakes, and the strawberries were long gone. And out in the grounds, holidaying parents lay under oaks, their faces hidden behind front pages, grateful that little Freddy or Ruby or Leon had stopped pestering for five minutes and had found the lawn skittles.

The heroes of this tale, however, weren't actually on holiday or anywhere near the garden. Twins Stella and Tom were hard at work. And luckily for them, they quite enjoyed it.

Since sneaking into the castle and making it their home,[1] Stella and Tom had been assistants to the caretaker, Harry Parkin (known to everyone as Parky) and lived with him in his cottage by the moat. You might think it is a bit strange for 10-year-old twins to work with a caretaker but until they arrived at the castle, Stella and Tom were totally alone in the world so they were only too happy to help look after it. At the castle, they polished the stately furniture, manned the till in the gift shop,

---

[1] See *The Twins, the Ghost and the Castle*, a laugh-out-loud read . . . highly recommended, apparently.

CHAPTER ONE

Holograms

"And this is the Duke of Wellington's very own room. He used to sleep here," Stella said with a sweep of her arms as she entered one of the rooms off the castle's main corridor, the flock of tourists waddling after her.

"The Duke of Wellington was Britain's most famous soldier," said Tom. "He defeated Napoleon at the battle of Waterloo in 1815."

"It's not very grand, is it?" clucked a tourist, wrinkling her nose at the sight of the poky, dimly lit quarters. "Hardly what you'd expect for a Duke."

"And that bed looks like it needs a right good scrubbing," added her husband, pointing to a fold-out cot in the corner.

Stella smiled, "The Duke might have been posh, but sometimes he still liked to live like a soldier. That's his army bed."

"Ugh, it looks it," fussed the wife. "Ghastly."

"What about the other rooms?" said the husband. "Something a bit more… you know, royal. We've got camping cots at home, you know." A few of the others honked in agreement.

Stella sighed – it had been one of those days. "Sure, come with me," she said leading the group down the corridor, "maybe you'll find Queen Victoria's room more interesting." She reached the Royal Room, turned the handle, and pushed open the door.

Then, there was a scream.

Not one of those 'ooh-isn't-the-water-cold' sort of screams, but a loud and horrifying wail that made everyone in the tour party want to hide. The tourists were all petrified, their throats tightening.

There, in the middle of the room, flickering ominously, was a cluster of ghosts. A terrifying and inexplicable squad of ghouls: a headmaster with a mortar board and cane, a sequined belly dancer, a devilish-looking centre forward, and a Roman legionary wearing full battle armour with a quiver of arrows embedded in his back. They were playing what looked to be a game of creepy, paranormal football using Queen Victoria's four-poster bed as a goal. To top it all off, refereeing the match was none other than the Duke of Wellington himself.

At the sight of the tour party, the spirits froze where they were, their ghostly football dropping to the floor, their eyes wide.

Then again came the scream – just as awful as before – from the mouth of the fussiest tourist, as she fainted away, her husband too stunned to catch her as she flumped onto the carpet. The others began to quiver and tremble.

Stella and Tom were speechless. Their mouths dropped open. What were the ghosts doing out? They were under strict instructions to stay hidden until closing time. Those were the rules.

"W-w-who in heaven's name are they?" gasped the husband, finding his voice (but still not bothering to help his wife).

"The undead," said another. "Mercy on our souls!"

"Run away!" cried a third, "they're going to possess us!"

Tom stepped in quickly. "Ah-ha-ha!" he laughed loudly, "No-no-no, those aren't the undead, those are our… our… our…" he jabbed his sister in the ribs.

"… our holograms," said Stella.

"Oh yes, holograms," said Tom. "We're still testing them out – very realistic aren't they? You can't even see the projectors."

"No projectors," said Stella.

"Holograms?" said the man, not quite convinced. He eyed the ghosts suspiciously, who were now doing their best to stand as still as marble.

"They're the latest thing," said Stella. "All the castles have them."

"They act out bits of history," said Tom. "See, if I press this switch here, the one that looks like the Duke of Wellington will tell you something very interesting." Tom flicked the light switch on the wall. The light in the room went on, and the apparition of the Duke of Wellington began to speak.

"Er, um, ah… welcome to my castle," the Duke intoned, causing the tour party to step back. "It's a grand castle isn't it? Very grand indeed," he paused. "Grand…" his voice trailed off. "Um, there's a pair of my famous boots around here somewhere, I think," said the Duke, looking a little lost. The tourists twittered at him.

"Hologram or not, he's not very good at tours," muttered the man, finally helping his wife to her feet. "And he's given Isadora a real fright." He patted his wife on the arm. "It's alright, love. They're just holograms – projections."

Stella glared at the Duke who was still umming and aahing and mumbling about nothing. "Yes, as we said, they're not quite ready yet." She turned the light switch off just as the Duke had thought of something good to say, and he fell silent again.

"I can understand why you've got the Duke of Wellington, he used to live here," said the wife when she'd regained her composure. "But why are there projections of that lot?" she asked, pointing to the footballer, the headmaster and the legionary. "And as for her," she gestured at the belly dancer, "she's downright inappropriate if you ask me. There's no call for jiggly bits in a historic building."

The belly dancer looked like she was about to say something in retort, but then thought better of it, and stood still.

"Goodness, is that the time?" said Tom, hastily pulling the group out of the room and closing the door. "And you still haven't seen the dining room!" he said, gesturing down the corridor.

"Are there holograms in there?" someone asked.

"Not in that room," said Stella quickly.

"No, not if they know what's good for them," muttered Tom.

CHAPTER TWO

Homesick

That evening, after the last of the visitors had driven off home down the coast, Parky called a meeting of all non-living castle personnel at six o'clock on the dot, in the drawing room. He was not a happy man.

Now, some people like to think that over time dog owners come to resemble their dogs. In Harry Parkin's case, a lifetime of looking after the castle had worked a similar spell on him. His face was worn and tender and had settled well into its age, like one of the castle's fine beechwood armchairs. His movements were slow and patient, infused with the stillness that hung about the ancient walls, his laugh, as soft as the Persian carpet in the corridor.

Little things he shared with the castle brought him private joy, like the creak of a certain floorboard under his feet, or the way the morning light crept over the rooms, gently waking them up when he pulled back the velvet curtains.

Generally speaking, Parky was a quiet and gentle soul. But disrupt his beloved home and its solitude, and you might see a different side to him. (As Mrs Crank from head office and her elaborate hairdo had once found out when she tried to change the castle into a beauty spa.) The ghosts all knew they had crossed the line that afternoon.

They gathered in the drawing room at a quarter to six, not daring to be late, and sat on (or rather half sank into) the maroon sofas and window seats that flanked the room. They waited in anxious silence as if they were in a doctors' surgery. All except for Marcus the Roman legionary, who still didn't really understand English, and wasn't exactly sure what was going on.

"Football," grumbled Headmaster Staines at last, glimmering with annoyance. "I blame you, Reg Butcher," he jabbed a finger at the football player.

"No one forced you," said the ghostly striker, rolling the spirit football that was often at his feet. "You've just got the hump because you were two goals down."

"We were not! That second was offside by a yard."

"Silence in the ranks!" ordered the Duke of Wellington – who when alive had been Field Marshal and Commander-in-Chief of his Majesty's forces, and so outranked the other ghosts in the castle by a mile. "Here they come."

Parky ambled into the room with the twins at his side, his face unmoving. If the ghosts had thought he would lose the plot and start shouting at them, they were wrong. Parky just slumped wearily into an armchair and let out a long, disappointed sigh. The ghosts looked at the floor in dismay. Disappointment was worse than shouting.

"When we rescued you from that ghost-catcher Stoneyheart and released you into the castle I thought we were clear about the rules," Parky sighed again. "Firstly, no dealings with the living. Secondly, no entering the public areas during the day," his voice rose just the tiniest bit, "and thirdly, *no* dealings with the living."

The ghosts all nodded guiltily.

"But for some quick thinking from these two," Parky continued, nodding at Stella and Tom, "the mess could have been a lot worse this afternoon. As it is, we've had one visitor faint dead away, two with an attack of nerves, and several with complaints to the head office about suspect holograms which are going to need some tricky explaining." Parky clenched his jaw. The ghosts avoided his eye.

The Duke of Wellington stood to attention and stared straight ahead. "As commanding officer, I take full responsibility for allowing our position to be known. It is my fault alone." He sat down.

"*Errare humanum est,*[2]" tried Marcus the legionary, holding up his hands (finally getting the gist of the conversation).

"Never mind that," said Stella with a kind smile, "why were you playing football in the first place?"

"I have to say, it was a major mistake," added Tom.

"It was foolhardy," the Duke agreed. "But it was in the interests of morale."

"Morale?" asked Parky.

The Duke looked at the other ghosts. "I was trying to inject a little camaraderie into the troops, a little *esprit de corps*. Mr Butcher here suggested a game of footy, and it seemed just the thing. We wrongly thought the last of the tourists had gone home."

"But why are you worried about morale?" asked Tom. "What's wrong?"

---

[2] To err is human. (That's Latin.)

14

The Duke looked again at the other ghosts, not sure whether to say or not.

Gelatina, the dancer, answered for him. "The truth is, Tom, we're feeling homesick, terribly so."

"All of us," admitted Headmaster Staines.

"We've been trying to hide it, but it's no use. His Grace was just trying to help." Gelatina winked at the Duke making him blush (well, as much as you can make a spirit of a long-dead soldier blush).

"Homesick?" said Stella. "But this castle has to be heaps better than being imprisoned in one of Stoneyheart's ghost traps."

"Certainly," said the headmaster. "And we're very grateful for being freed." The other ghosts agreed.

"But no matter how hard we try to forget it, this castle just ain't home," said Reg the footballer. "And that's the difference. What I would give to be haunting the turf of Grungely Park again," he sighed.

"To tread the boards at the Theatre Majestic," said Gelatina.

"To walk the hallowed halls of Strapping Manor," added the headmaster.

"*Domus, dulcis, domus*," agreed Marcus.

"Home, sweet, home," the Duke translated helpfully.

"If only there was some sort of railway for ghosts," said Gelatina. "We could take it home."

Now, Parky's creased brow softened as the irritation drained away. He glanced around the motley crew of spirits who had somehow become his responsibility. How could he be cross with them? Ghosts or not, it was no fun being homesick, as he remembered from his days at boarding school.

He got to his feet, smiling in what he hoped was a caring way. "I'm sorry – I really had no idea. But these things often pass with time, surely?" Parky said brightly.

"Well, that's one thing we *do* have," said Reg Butcher, "all the blinking time in the world."

"Well, goodnight everyone, goodnight your Grace," Parky said to the Duke.

But Wellington was lost in his own thoughts. Something Gelatina had said was giving him pause…

CHAPTER THREE

"The game's afoot"

As another day at the castle by the sea ended, Stella and Tom were finishing the last of their long list of jobs. Stella was giving a final polish to the statue of Wellington's head and shoulders, his bold features carved out of white marble, when the eyes of the statue suddenly opened. She jumped back with a yelp.

"All clear?" whispered the Duke of Wellington, giving her a wink.

Stella took a hurried look around. There were no tourists left on the landing. "I wish you wouldn't lie in wait and pop out like that," she hissed. "You gave me a fright."

"Sorry, but after yesterday, I thought it wisest to have a quick dekko[3] around the place before I stuck my neck out," the Duke peered around the hallway. "I need to see you and Tom on a

---

[3] From the Hindi *dekho*, meaning to have a look, a gander, a *shufti*, a peek, a look-see.

matter of most urgency. Can't say more at the moment." He winked again. "But suffice to say, the game's afoot. Shall we say my quarters in an hour?"

* * *

"What's going on?" asked Tom when they met in Wellington's room.

"Bring down that map book if you please," said the Duke pointing to one of the many books on his shelves. "And locate me a good one of Britain."

Tom did what he was told, and found a page that showed the whole kingdom, drawn neatly in black ink on paper that had begun to yellow. The twins were used to getting books for the Duke and turning pages, as being a ghost he couldn't pick up anything, which he found most annoying.

The Duke peered over at the map. "Yes, yes," he said with some enthusiasm, "it shouldn't be too hard at all really," he allowed his finger to trace its way over various squiggles and lines. "Rutupiae first, followed by here, then there, then a quick jaunt up there, and lastly back down to here," he mumbled to himself. "Nothing to it."

"Nothing to what?" asked Stella.

"The grand tour," said Wellington. "For ghosts. I have it all worked out. We'll do it in the castle's automated conveyance."

"Automated conveyance?" asked Tom.

"He means the minibus," said Stella, having quickly realised what the Duke was on about. "You're planning a trip to take all the ghosts back to their old homes, aren't you?"

The Duke beamed. "Precisely. Gelatina's idea about a ghost railway yesterday got me thinking."

"But how will we get everyone onto the bus?" Tom pointed out. "You know ghosts can't move from one haunting to another."

"But they can, and the answer's been right under our noses this whole time," said the Duke tapping his rather large beak. "Follow me."

The twins chased after the Duke as he swept his way eagerly down the stairs, out through the gift shop and into the gatehouse. There he melted through a small door marked 'storage' and disappeared.

"Well, come on then," came his muffled voice through the wood.

Tom tried several keys from his caretaker's key chain until he found the right one, and with a groan, the door swung open.

"There's a light switch over there," said the Duke, his shape glowing in the darkness.

Stella flicked on the light, and they found themselves in a tiny storeroom filled with all manner of junk.

"Up there," said the Duke pointing to one of the shelves. "We'll only need one of them to start with."

The twins followed Wellington's gaze. There on the shelf were four black containers, each about the size of a shoebox, with buttons and dials along one side. At one end of each container was what looked like a kitchen funnel.

"Stoneyheart's ghost-catching traps!" said Stella. "I remember now, he left them behind when he ran away."

The three of them gave a little chuckle recalling how Seymour Stoneyheart, professional ghost-catcher and all-round nasty piece of work, had run for his life the last time he had set foot in the castle. His plan to capture the ghost of the Duke of Wellington had ended up in something of a mess.

Tom found a small stepladder and reached one of the boxes down. "Of course! Stoneyheart's boxes. We can use these to grab the ghosts and move them onto the bus. If we release the ghosts into the bus they can haunt the bus for a little while, right?"

The Duke nodded, "Precisely. We can make the bus a temporary haunting, journey about the country and use the boxes again to move each ghost back to their original homes."

"Any idea if they still work?" said Stella eyeing the dials and knobs.

"There's only one way to find out," said the Duke.

Tom carried the ghost trap upstairs with the others at his heels, and found a socket in Wellington's room. He cautiously plugged it in and pressed the power button. A red light on the top began to blink. "Now what?"

Stella blew the dust off the controls and studied them for a bit. "It should be simple really, there is one switch called 'capture' and one that says 'release'."

"Are you sure you really want to do this?" said Tom.

"Someone has to test it out," said the Duke. "A good leader leads by example."

"What if we make a mistake and you somehow disappear forever?" asked Stella.

"*There is no mistake; there has been no mistake; and there shall be no mistake,*[4]" said the Duke. "We need to get our friends home, and this is the way. Press the button, if you will."

Holding her breath and wincing slightly, Stella leaned over and pressed the 'capture' switch. There was a whining and a whirring from inside the box, then a sucking sound came from the funnel, not unlike a vacuum cleaner. The box started to vibrate.

The Duke began to flicker, faintly at first, but then he got more and more jerky and disjointed – like a video full of glitches. Suddenly his legs disappeared into the funnel like smoke, then his torso went, and finally, before he could say goodbye, his head vanished into nothing. In an instant, the Duke had ceased to exist.

Stella and Tom looked at each other. Their friend was gone.

---

[4] Wellington really said those words, or is thought to have said them…

Chapter Four

"All present and accounted for"

Having successfully entered the box and come back again without so much as a scratch, the Duke spent the next few days planning the tour with military precision. He hadn't looked forward to something so much for at least 161 and a ½ years. Using a modern road map ("Good lord! Where have all the woods gone?") he carefully stored the route in his head, and worked out the plan of attack. Getting each ghost safely back into their original hauntings without detection was something that needed cautious handling.

After getting used to the idea, Parky had to admit he was looking forward to having a little trip himself. He and the twins hadn't really had a holiday in all the time since they'd moved in. For their part, the ghostly crew couldn't have been happier. At long last, they were going home. After spending many dark years imprisoned inside the ghost traps, and then more months in a castle where they didn't really fit in, they were finally going back where they belonged. With the minibus as a stopgap haunting, they would take a grand tour together, a grand, ghostly tour, back to each of their homes, one by one.

First stop on the tour would be the ruins of Richborough, known in the Roman days as Rutupiae, last known whereabouts of Marcus the legionary. They would sneak out that evening.

"Rutupiae?" Marcus asked when the twins were trying to explain what was going on. He eyed the funnel of the ghost trap with dread.

"Rutupiae," said Tom. "*Veritas.*[5]"

"*Bene*," Marcus nodded stepping up to the box. "Good," he said in English, and Stella turned the dial to 'capture'.

The rest of the ghosts were already packed and waiting (not that they had anything to pack, of

---

[5] Truth, true

25

course) and cheered from their seats when Marcus burst into the minibus.

"Here he is!" said Reg Butcher calling out from the back. "I saved you a seat for the grand tour, me old mucker!"

"All present and accounted for," said the Duke from the passenger's seat when Tom slid the door closed. "You may proceed, Mr Parkin."

"Right you are," said Parky, and the wheels of the minibus crunched happily on the gravel and down the tree-lined drive.

If Wellington hadn't been so excited to get underway, and the tour party hadn't been quite so full of life, they might have noticed the oil-slick of a man hiding in the trees, with a face like a scorched steam iron. Seymour Stoneyheart, ghost-catcher, joy-killer, and all-round nasty piece of work, couldn't believe his luck.

Ever since that horrendous episode at the castle the previous year, when Parky and the Duke - he corrected himself – when Parky and *it* (ghosts were never people, they were always '*it*') had rallied the other ghouls and sent him packing, Stoneyheart had been set on revenge. A bit of 'ghost-napping' was in order. He would abduct the apparition of Wellington, make him a crowning addition to his ghostly trophy collection, and trap him there until the end of time. Payback.

So, for the past week, Stoneyheart had prowled the castle grounds, concealed in the woods, shrouded in his dark suit, dark hat, dark socks, dark trilby pulled down low, waiting for the right moment to sneak in and catch the foul ghoul. But it had proved trickier than he'd first thought. There were just so many tourists around, not to mention that man Parky and those two children of his who seemed to be everywhere.

Now, though, was his chance. With the ghosts on the move (and they were using his own ghost traps as well – infuriating!), they were sure to drop their guard at some point. He just needed to wait for the right moment. Stoneyheart scampered through the castle gates to his van parked by the side of the road, his hands shaking as he turned the key and started it up.

Dusk was dropping down over the darkening sea as the castle minibus rumbled down the road, heading inland away from the coast. The ghosts were thrilled by the sight of the countryside speeding past, the old oak trees, the distant lights of ships out in the channel, the church spires reaching up into the evening sky. Wellington, being a more practical sort, was wondering about the minibus.

27

"This is quite something," he said, eyebrow raised, watching as Parky changed gears. "The power of one hundred and eighty-eight horses you say?" Parky nodded.

"At the roundabout, take the first left," purred the satnav from the dashboard.

The Duke sat upright. "Who said that?" he muttered, looking around.

Parky chuckled. "It's our satnav – a satellite navigation system." He tapped the screen. "I call her Bridget. I always have her on."

Wellington eyed the tiny device with misgiving. "Navigation? But I have the journey already planned, we don't need her meddling in our affairs."

"In one hundred feet, turn left!" said Bridget.

"Now, steady on!" the Duke wagged a finger at Bridget. "I'm in command here."

"Turn left!" said Bridget again. Parky indicated, and turned.

"Madam, I'll have you court-martialled for insubordination!" warned the Duke.

"Drive straight for 10.5 miles," said Bridget, not paying him the slightest attention.

"Court-martialled!" roared the Duke, his face going red.

"This trip's going to be fun," Parky laughed.

Stuck to their tail several car lengths behind, his eyes narrowed, rotten villainy on his mind, Stoneyheart changed gear, pulling the van closer. The ghost-catcher wasn't usually one for jollity, his features were mostly set to 'sour and bitter'. But now the hint of a chuckle escaped from his throat. It felt good to be back on the hunt.

"I'm coming to get you, ghostie," he hissed, putting his foot down.

CHAPTER FIVE

One down

The tour party reached Richborough as the last of the day ebbed away, but there was just enough light to make out the remains of the fort walls, stretching out along the field like ancient guards of stone and flint. A series of deep, grassy ditches surrounded the fort, and just outside, lay a small cottage, its lights glowing.

At the sight of the ruins, Marcus's face shone. "Rutupiae," he whispered.

"We'll have to be careful, now," said Parky pulling the minibus to a stop. "Gordon, the caretaker, is in. He's a mate, but all the same, no need for him to know."

"Best we sneak Marcus in through the West Gate," said the Duke, pointing to a gap in the walls well away from the cottage.

"Are you sure you really want to get out?" Stella asked Marcus. "It doesn't look very welcoming," she pointed out at the windswept site.

"You could always stay on at the castle with us," Tom agreed.

Marcus smiled and shook his head. Though he didn't know the words, he understood what the children were saying. He tapped his breastplate, and pointed at the fort. "*Domus*," he said with a grin.

No sooner had Marcus said the word 'home' than Stella spotted a flickering glow, by the West Gate, the very spot the Duke had mentioned. But it wasn't just a single glow, it was a whole lot of glowing shapes, and if Stella wasn't mistaken, they were heading towards them.

"Troops on the march," said the Duke from the front seat. "I'd recognise that anywhere."

"Looks like your mates are here, Marcus," said Reg.

The occupants of the minibus watched with great interest as the Roman patrol marched in formation along the outside of the wall, spears and shields in hand, cloaks wrapped over their shoulders.

"Aren't they smashing?" said Gelatina.

"If I'm not mistaken, they are what were known in the Roman army as a *contubernium*, a squad

31

of eight men, tent mates if you like," Headmaster Staines pointed out.

Tom did a quick count, "but there are only seven of them."

"No doubt that's where our friend comes in," said the headmaster.

Marcus nodded vigorously, pointed to himself again, and then pointed at the soldiers. The patrol carried on marching and disappeared around the corner.

"We'd better get you back there, then," said Parky, reaching for a ghost trap. "Give us a hand, Stella."

The ghosts quickly made their farewells. "He'd have made one cracking centre back," said Reg with a sigh, as Marcus disappeared into the trap.

The twins and Parky climbed over the low fence surrounding the property, and made their way down into one of the grassy ditches and up the other side. Walking as quickly and as silently as they could, they rounded the corner and then broke into a run, racing after the fast-receding soldiers.

"Catch them, Tom," Parky gasped.

Tom sprinted ahead and circled round the front of the patrol. Not that he would ever admit it to Stella, but up close, the legionaries were just a little bit terrifying. He closed his eyes and thrust out his hand in front of him. Immediately, the patrol came to a stop, feet clomping, shields and javelins clattering. (All except the legionary at the back who wasn't paying attention, and walked right through the soldier in front and got a bit stuck.)

The leader of the patrol drew his sword and glared down at Tom, letting off a rattle of Latin as Stella and Parky caught up.

"Let me do the talking," said Parky. "*Me excusa*," Parky held up his hands in apology. "*Semper ubi, sub ubi,*[6]" he said, smiling.

The leader of the patrol looked puzzled. He turned to the others and muttered something, chuckling. There was a collective shrugging of shoulders.

Parky cleared his throat and tried again. "Er... *ubi sunt latrinae*?[7]" and the whole patrol burst into laughter, their armour rattling with amusement.

Parky looked at the ground. "Oh dear, I should have paid better attention in school."

"Better just let Marcus out, before your Latin gets the caretaker's attention," laughed Stella, putting the box down and setting it to 'release'.

---

[6] Always where under where… always wear underwear, geddit?
[7] Where's the toilet?

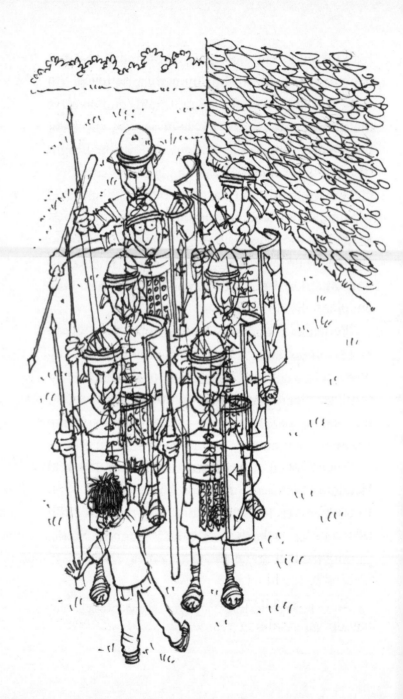

Skulking around in the gloom, out of sight behind a Roman wall, Stoneyheart watched the little reunion, his face in a sneer. So, releasing the ghosts were they? The ghost-catcher ground his teeth – those ghosts should be boxed up, decorating his mantelpiece. Those foul muddles of electromagnetic energy didn't deserve to be free.

Stoneyheart sniggered as the legionaries huddled around sharing news, trying to shake hands and slap backs (which was hard to do when they could not touch anything). The twins and Parky looked on, pleased with themselves.

"Pathetic," scoffed Stoneyheart. He could always come back and trap the legionaries some other time, but right now he needed to keep his eye on the main prize. When the moment was right, he'd attack. Stoneyheart crept away, back to his van, a wicked glow in his eyes.

When Parky and the twins got back to the minibus, Headmaster Staines was wrapping up his lecture on Roman history, politely ignoring Reg who had been asleep in the back for quite some time.

"How did it go?" asked Gelatina. "Were they pleased to see him?"

"It was like a family reunion," said Parky. "They couldn't stop talking, *tempus*, this and *quid* that."

"Oh, how nice!" said Gelatina.

"Just think, that'll be you tomorrow," said Stella, and Gelatina beamed.

The Duke took out his pocket watch. "Well, one down, three to go. So far, so good. We'll stop here for the night, and make for Gelatina's theatre in the morning. Reg's got the right idea," he said, gesturing at the sleeping footballer.

"Fair enough," said Parky. "An early night it is."

Parky and the twins got out their sleeping bags and pillows, laying them out on the rows of seats as best they could. The ghosts curled up where there was space. Being spirits they didn't really mind if they had to make do with the hard floor. Parky got out the picnic hamper and handed the twins their sandwiches for dinner, and a cold mug of juice from the flask.

"Just like camping," said Stella.

"Ah, there's nothing quite like it," said the Duke, thinking of all his time spent under canvas.

It made for a cosy scene, the twins and Parky resting on their sleeping bags in the minibus, the summer breeze creeping through the open windows, as the walls of the ancient fort caught the moonlight. They lay in silence, happily watching the stars.

Tom broke the quiet. "Gelatina, if you don't mind me asking, how did you... you know..."

"Pass away?" Gelatina said finishing his sentence.

"Tom!" Stella was horrified. "That's rude."

"Just wondering," said Tom.

"That's alright, I don't mind. It was quite something." Gelatina thought for a moment. "I was appearing in a panto, Ali Baba and the Forty Thieves. I had the part of Morgiana the beautiful and clever servant – of course, I was perfect for the part," Gelatina sighed. "Well, anyway, the show climaxed in a wild Raqs Sharqi – a traditional dance – what some people call a belly dance. I did all the choreography myself in those days. For the grand finale, I was to leap off a high balcony and into Ali Baba's arms. It was going to be a showstopper. Only thing was that on the night, Ali Baba went *left*, and I leapt *right*. Turns out the actor playing Ali Baba didn't know one hand from the other."

"Ouch," Tom winced.

"Yes, I flew headfirst into the orchestra pit." Gelatina broke into giggles. "You could say Ali Baba *left* me in a *right* mess."

The minibus shook with laughter. Tom rolled his eyes, finally getting the joke. "Ha, ha, *left*, *right*, very funny. How did you *really* pass away?" he said, shaking his head.

"I had a nap one day backstage in-between shows and didn't wake up," said Gelatina.

"I prefer the other story," said Stella.

"Me too." Gelatina smiled. "I tell you, I can't wait to make my entrance tomorrow."

CHAPTER SIX

"O Romeo, Romeo! Wherefore art thou Romeo?"

"Now, there's no need to have *her* involved," said the Duke the following morning, as they were setting off from the fort. He jabbed his finger at the satnav. "I know this part of the country like the back of my hand. Take this left, here."

After going round in loops and ending up at the same little village for the third time, Parky switched Bridget back on.

"In 1.5 miles turn right," said Bridget, with a tone of slight disdain.

"It's only because there are all these roundabouts littering up the place," grumbled the Duke.

It was a good job Bridget was switched on – when they finally got to the town by the sea, they badly needed her help to find the Theatre Majestic in amongst the rambling streets. Bridget guided their way through a web of deserted lanes, up and down hills, and around corners. They eventually found the timeworn theatre down one of the back streets, the name lit up cheerfully on the curved, white façade of the building.

"She never fails to give me a tingle down my spine. Can you smell the magic in the air? Feel the irresistible pull of the stage?" Gelatina's face glowed. "Go round the back, if you would be so kind, Mr Parkin."

Parky pulled in down the narrow alley and brought the minibus to a stop by the stage entrance. A dark van parked around the corner behind them. "Do you think there'll be anyone in?"

"Not a living soul, not at this time in the morning, anyway. It's ages before the matinee. Now, you'll find the spare key under that loose brick there," Gelatina pointed to the step. She turned to the other ghosts. "Now, I don't do goodbyes, luvvies. Just a simple peck on the cheek."

"Break a leg," said Headmaster Staines, as Tom got the ghost trap ready.

The key was where Gelatina said it would be, and with a creaking of rusty hinges, the twins and

Parky opened the door and quickly slipped into the theatre. Inside, it was dark and smelt of damp.

"I'm not sure it's magic I smell in the air," Tom sniffed.

"Anyone bring a torch?" asked Stella.

"No, but there's light coming from over there," said Tom. He was right, a faint glow made its way down the stairs, bringing with it the sound of voices.

"Tiptoe," said Parky, holding his finger to his lips. He didn't fancy them being nabbed for breaking and entering.

The three of them crawled up the stairs like mice, (three blind mice, if you'll excuse a rather feeble joke), towards the light. At the top of the stairs, behind the stage wings, they stopped and listened. It sounded like they'd turned up right in the middle of a rehearsal.

"I thought Gelatina said it would be empty," whispered Stella.

Tom shrugged and gently pulled back the curtain. There on stage shimmered two actors, two ghostly actors, in full costume, a third watching on from the empty theatre. "She did say not a *living* soul."

Now one of the actors held his arm up to the heavens and thrust out his chest, his voice clear and proud.

41

"But, soft! what light through yonder window breaks?
It is the east, and Juliet is the sun.
Arise, fair sun, and kill the envious moon…"

He did a little spin in his leotards.

"That's Romeo," whispered Stella from behind the curtain.

"You know him?" asked Tom, surprised.

"*Romeo and Juliet* – it's Shakespeare,[8]" murmured Stella.

"Oh," said Tom.

Now the other actor cut in, his high-pitched voice screeching through the darkness. *"O Romeo, Romeo! Wherefore art thou Romeo?"* Stella and Tom winced.

"No, no, no!" the third ghost called out from the theatre, stopping the play dead. He marched up to the stage. "This won't do at all! Juliet, you've fluffed it."

"Oh dear," said the actor playing Juliet. "Too soon?"

"Far too soon," said the director.

---

[8] William Shakespeare 1564-1616. Also known as Bill; the Bard; possibly the greatest writer in the English language; you know… the man with the beard, the earring and the funny collar.

"Once again, you've ruined my monologue," sniffed Romeo.

"Sorry," said Juliet.

The director shook his head. "Besides, dearest, Juliet is meant to be an angel, a delicate rose, the sweetest of maidens..."

"... and not a suffering, old goat!" said Romeo.

Juliet looked down at his shoes, hurt. "It's not my fault – I can't do a woman's voice. I get all flustered."

"More's the pity," the director sighed.

Stella nudged Tom in the ribs. "I think that's her cue."

Tom turned the switch, and immediately Gelatina burst out onto the stage, a cloud of steam surrounding her like a crown. The other ghosts froze, but the astonished looks on their faces rapidly changed from those of panic to those of delight.

"Gelatina!" said one.

"Gelatina!" said the other.

"Finally, a Juliet!" said the director. "Thank heavens!"

Gelatina threw open her arms. "Darlings," she warbled, prancing towards them from stage left. "Now tell me, wasn't that simply the best entrance you've ever seen?"

When they got back, the twins and Parky found
the others playing 'I Spy.'

"I spy with my little eye, something beginning
with T," said Reg.

"Theatre," said the Duke. "You've already done
that one."

"Have I?" said Reg.

"Twice."

"How'd you get on?" asked Headmaster Staines.

"Great," said Parky.

"We even met Romeo and Juliet," said Tom.

"Ah, the Bard," said Headmaster Staines, a dreamy look in his eye. And as Parky started up the minibus for Strapping Manor, the old headmaster began to recite:

"Two households, both alike in dignity,
In fair Verona, where we lay our scene,
From ancient grudge break to new mutiny..."

... and off they went.

Chapter Seven

Gibber, jabber

Strapping Manor Grammar turned out to be a towering, old pile, with walls of hard brick and a gloomy, slate roof. A thick door blocked the entrance. The halls of the school formed three sides of a square, and in the middle was an area of ground where the students could play games – if it hadn't been for the signs saying, 'no games in the quad,' in big, red letters.

"Yuck," Stella whispered to Tom, not wanting to hurt Headmaster Staines's feelings. "This place doesn't look like any fun."

"Ah, the blessed halls of the Manor, home of the fortunate few," said the headmaster with a sigh as they passed the school and parked down the street. "Can't wait to get back to my desk."

"Now, what's the plan to get inside?" Parky asked as he turned off the ignition. "Do we wait until the end of the school day?"

The Duke shook his head. "It's simpler than that. The headmaster and I have it worked out. You just tell reception that you're new to the area and would like a tour. Then, when they're not looking, one of you sneaks off round the corner and releases the headmaster."

"That *is* simple," agreed Parky.

When the three of them had left, the Duke and Reg found themselves waiting in the minibus again.

"Well, I could use a toes-up myself," Reg said, flopping over and lying down. "Seeing as tomorrow's a match day."

"Agreed," said the Duke stretching himself out on the seat. "I find all this travelling by automated conveyance rather tiring." It did not take long for the two friends to drop off to sleep, each giving off little ghostly snores.

Perhaps if they had seen the dark van behind them parked on the same side of the street, and seen who was in its front seat, they would not have slept so easily. Watching them through binoculars was Stoneyheart.

47

The ghost-catcher cracked his knuckles. This was it. Until now, it had been just too chancy to make his move. Not at the fort, not at the theatre. There was too much risk of being rumbled, and too many other ghouls to contend with. (He thought back to the way his friend Mrs Crank from the castle had been cruelly possessed by the belly dancer.) Now there were only two apparitions left in the van and it looked like they were both asleep. Perfect. He'd have to be quick – break into the van and nab the Duke without getting into a tussle with the ghost of Reg Butcher, without arousing anyone's suspicions, without anyone seeing. Tricky, but possible.

Stoneyheart slid open the side door of his van, and chose a ghost trap from the equipment hanging neatly in the back. A wide funnel, for catching ghosts, was attached to the side of the ghost trap. He undid this funnel and attached a long nozzle – a bit like the hose on a vacuum cleaner. It would be easier to slip the hose in through the minibus window. Stoneyheart closed the van door and walked towards the minibus, as calmly as he could manage. Time to strike. Ghost-napping time.

Then Stoneyheart stopped, and started to back away. A shifty weasel of a man, a metal bar in his hand, was fiddling with the front door of the castle minibus at that very moment, trying very hard to look low-key while he did it.

"Car thief!" Stoneyheart growled. Just what he needed, a filthy, little robber. Stoneyheart crept back to his van with a face like a bruise. Now he would just have to sit tight and see what happened next.

The truth was, the car thief was only a burglar in training, as he had never actually stolen a car before. In fact, as he fiddled with the minibus lock, he was beginning to wonder if he was cut out for it at all.

He was about to slip his metal bar down the gap between the window and the door, when he noticed that the minibus wasn't even locked. "Wahey," the thief said aloud, quietly opening the door. He glanced up and down the street to see if anyone had noticed, but no one had.

The man reached under the steering wheel and yanked out the ignition wires, flicking the ends of the red and yellow ones together the way he'd seen them do it in films. For the first time ever, it actually worked. The minibus stuttered to life, engine rumbling. The man hopped into the driver's seat, took another quick look around, and pulled away from the curb.

"Turn right, then turn right."

At the sound of a voice, the thief jumped back, heart pounding. "Don't do that!" Annoyed, he pressed the 'off' switch on the satnav. "Scared me half to death."

"Turn right!"

"Quiet, you," said the man, pressing at the controls.

"Turn right!"

"I've got a good mind to chuck you out the window," the man hissed.

Then, there came another voice from inside the minibus. From the passenger seats. From the supposedly empty passenger seats.

"I would leave Bridget alone if I were you!" said the voice.

This time, the thief's heart almost left his body.

He swivelled round, nearly sending the minibus off the road. "Aaagh!" he yelped, quickly swerving the minibus back. It couldn't be. He was losing it. He could swear there was someone in the back. And that someone looked like a ghost. A ghost? No chance. The man closed his eyes for a second, hoping it had gone away. Then, coming to a stop at the lights, he got up the courage to peer in the rear-view mirror.

Whatever it was had gone. The man let out a long breath. He instantly decided he really couldn't handle being a thief. Thieving was making him see and hear things. He would sell this one minibus and pack it in. He put the minibus in gear again, and lurched away from the lights.

"Looking for me?" came the voice. And there he was in front of him. A head, rising up through the dashboard. A ghostly head. And it looked annoyed. The robber screamed, slammed both his trainers down on the brakes, and the minibus skidded to a stop with a screeching of tyres. He gripped the steering wheel, not daring to move. Behind him came the angry blaring of horns.

"That's better," said the Duke, rising up a little more. "Now turn us round, and take us back to where we came from," he ordered.

The thief was stiff as a floorboard. "G-g-gibber," he said, finally.

"Back to where we came from, there's a good lad," tried the Duke again.

"J-j-jabber," spluttered the thief.

Reg sat up in the back seat, stretching his arms. "What's going on?" he yawned.

"This ruffian here is trying to steal our automated conveyance," said the Duke.

"We can't have that," said Reg.

"No, we can't," agreed the Duke.

The man groaned, his face pale, his mouth opening and closing like a blowfish.

"What've you done to him?" asked Reg. "He looks poorly."

"I'm getting quite good at haunting," the Duke smiled.

"Gibber?" whined the robber.

Reg looked around at the traffic. The blaring of horns was getting louder and more heated. "We'd better do something sharpish, this lot are doing their nut in," he gestured at the cars. "We don't want them taking a closer look."

"He's right, you know," said the Duke to the car thief. "Get a move on!"

"Jabber," whimpered the thief gazing into space, eyes blank. "Gibber."

"Pah, his mind's gone. There's nothing for it!" said the Duke, slipping into the car thief's body. "Time to take control."

Parky and the twins came out of Strapping Manor feeling pleased with themselves. Headmaster Staines was back haunting his old school like he had never left. Then their happy feeling evaporated in an instant. Kangarooing up the street, engine complaining, brakes squealing, gears crunching, was the castle minibus – with a strange man gripping the wheel. The minibus shuddered to a stop on the curb outside the school and then the man turned and waved at them.

"Tally-ho!" he called out. "Your automated conveyance awaits!"

The twins and Parky gaped. "That sounded just like his Grace," said Parky slowly.

"Only he doesn't look like him," said Tom.

The strange man waved at them again. "*Up and at 'em* if you please, no time to waste!"

"And the magical, mystery tour takes on a whole new level of strangeness… " said Stella, shaking her head.

CHAPTER EIGHT

One-nil to the Fusiliers

The following morning on the drive up to London, the Duke was still full of himself. "I could take over for a while, if you get tired, Mr Parkin," he offered.

"You're not possessing me," said Parky. "That man was a wreck after we left him yesterday."

"But just think, he'll never steal anything ever again," Stella pointed out.

"That's true."

"And the look on his face when he ran off, you'd think he'd seen a ghost," laughed Tom.

"At the roundabout take the second exit... exit left," purred Bridget.

"Right you are," said the Duke.

"I hope she knows how to get us to Grungely Park, I don't want to be late for kick-off!" said Reg from the back, bouncing up and down. "Can't miss kick-off."

As the castle minibus made its way across London, Bridget certainly earned her keep, taking them along little-known backstreets and alleys, not putting a wheel wrong. The closer they got to Grungely Park, the home of Fusiliers F.C., the more worked up Reg became. Once they crossed the river, he pointed out little landmarks to the twins in a flurry of commentary, like the registry office where he had got married, his favourite fish and chip shop (which was still going), and the tiny park where he had first learned to kick a football.

But while Reg kept up his excited patter, at each passing street the Duke became ever more silent. He hadn't been back to London in over 150 years, and the capital which he thought he knew so well was unrecognisable. So when the minibus stopped down a side street a short walk from Grungely Park, the Duke made his mind up not to get out.

"But there'll be plenty of places to hide and watch the match," argued Tom.

"No one will even notice," said Stella. "Come on."

"It's bound to be a cracking contest," said Reg.

The Duke waved them away. "After yesterday's shenanigans I think it best I guard over the minibus," he lied. He stuck out his hand. "Reg Butcher, it has been a pleasure making your acquaintance, and I wish you the very best."

Reg bowed. "If you're ever up this neck of the woods again, promise me you won't be shy."

The Duke nodded. "Now, off you go, or you'll miss the whistle."

* * *

Stoneyheart was furious with himself. Yesterday, that fool car thief had got in the way just when he was making his move, and now with all the twisting and turning the castle minibus had been doing, he was lost in the backstreets.

"I'll never find them with all this traffic," Stoneyheart grumbled to himself. How could he catch up again?

Stoneyheart pulled his van over and gave it some thought. So far, each ghost was back at its original haunting. The legionary at its Roman fort, the belly dancer at its theatre, the headmaster at its school. So where might they be going with the ghost Wellington? *Its* home was the castle by the sea, wasn't it?

Then Stoneyheart had it. Of course. When Wellington was alive he had several homes, and one famous one right in the middle of London. Stoneyheart knew exactly where Parky and the twins were headed, and this time he would be lying in wait.

* * *

The mighty ground of Grungely Park was a sea of red and white as Reg had promised. Stand after stand, seat after seat, was filled with fan after chanting fan, thousands of voices soaring into the city sky, drowning out the pitiful section of away supporters in the corner.

"And it's Fusiliers,
Fusiliers, F.C. ...
We're by far the greatest team the world has ever seen... "

As the twins and Parky picked their way through the stand and found their seats, the teams came out of the tunnel to an eruption of noise. All eyes were on the pitch, on the team in red and white, and their opponents in blue, and not a single fan had noticed the ghostly apparition of Reg Butcher sitting in his seat.

The handshakes between the teams were quickly over and, with a look at his watch, the ref gave a sharp blast from his whistle.

"Come on, Fusiliers!" Reg bellowed.

But it soon became clear, that no matter how much thundering and cheering and scarf waving went on, Fusiliers F.C. weren't playing well. Untidy passes, wild shots which ended up in row Z, crosses which ballooned into touch. Fusiliers were spent and lifeless, and with ten minutes before the final whistle, they were barely holding on.

Everyone watching could tell the home side were creaking – Walters in goal was the only one keeping them in it. To make matters worse, a nasty challenge sent Fusiliers' striker Justinho clattering to the ground where he lay crumpled in a pile.

"Foul!" shouted Reg.

The ref got out his yellow card for the defender in blue, and Justinho was stretchered off. Everyone watched fearfully as the Brazilian received treatment. The ref restarted the match, with the Fusiliers down to ten men.

"He looks dazed," said Tom pointing at Justinho.

"The manager needs to bring on some fresh legs," said Parky.

"Or breathe some life into old ones," Reg declared, standing up. "Thanks for everything you lot, don't be strangers will you?" he said and he ran down the stairs.

"Here we go again," sighed Stella.

Down on the pitch, the team physio was about to let the manager know that Justinho wasn't fit to carry on, when the Brazilian sat bolt upright on the grass and jumped to his feet.

"Let's go then!" he cried, thumping his chest, the crowd thundering their approval.

The official waved Justinho on.

Up in the stands, Parky and the twins were dumbfounded. Had they been the only ones to notice Reg as he climbed into the injured footballer? Stella asked the man next to her to turn up his radio, and leaned in to listen.

"Fusiliers looked dead and buried a moment ago, but Justinho seems to have found an extra burst of energy from somewhere, John."

"I didn't think he was going to come back on to be honest."

"And here he is now, pressing high up the pitch, driving his teammates. Justinho… to Fredericks… back to Justinho, a nice little one-two. A flick on to Edwards, the crowd impatient, urging him on."

"Edwards holding the ball up nicely, takes it past Roberts – and picks up Justinho, free

in space, lovely first touch. Justinho nutmegs Terrence... Justinho... JUSTINHO!"

"GOOOOOAAAAL!"

The entire stadium rose to their feet screaming.

"Well Frank, out of nowhere, a fabulous, fabulous goal."

"You can say that again, John. A goal of real individual brilliance. The game needed someone to step up and take charge, and Justinho's done just that. Even the great Reg Butcher would have been proud of that one... "

"I bet he is," said Stella.

"One-nil to the Fusiliers," cheered Tom, joining in with the crowd.

CHAPTER NINE

Number One, London

Stella, Tom and Parky were pulled along by the mass of still-chanting fans and out onto the street. After their shredded nerves, hot dogs seemed to be the order of the day, and the siren song of fried onions and sausages drifted over the supporters calling them forward.

"Fancy one?" asked Parky pointing to a food cart. "Or is that a silly question?"

Munching away on their sausages, the three of them found their way back to the castle minibus, and a gloomy looking passenger staring blankly out of the window.

The Duke raised his head and forced a smile onto his lips. "I take it from the boisterous celebrations the Fusiliers were victorious?"

"Thanks to a little help from Reg," said Tom.

"He's back at home," said Parky, "but I nearly had a heart attack. Gives a whole new meaning to 'possession football.' Hope he doesn't do that again."

"Good, good," said the Duke.

"So, mission accomplished!" said Tom.

"I guess we can head off home," added Stella. Then she saw the look on the Duke's face. He looked a little like a lost child. "Is anything wrong?" she asked.

"No, no," said the Duke. "Nothing of any note, anyway."

"Go on, tell," said Tom.

Wellington paused for a moment, then let out a long breath. "It's just that I was so looking forward to our trip to London. So looking forward… "

"And?" asked Parky.

"This isn't London. Not the London I knew."

"Well it has been a while," said Tom.

"That's just it. Everything changes, while I'm still stuck in the past, completely out of step. I don't suppose I noticed it so much before." There was a silence in the minibus, as no one really had an answer to that. "Best I get back to the castle by the sea," said the Duke bravely. "To the little corner where I belong."

But Parky had thought of something. A way of perhaps making things better. "No need to rush, is there? We are on a sort of holiday, aren't we? There's one more stop I'd like to make. I think you might approve, your Grace." Parky started the minibus, and then scrolled through Bridget's console.

"Where are we off to?" asked Stella. But Parky just winked and tapped his nose.

"Turn left," said Bridget, yawning. "Turn left."

"Just for once, can't she say 'hello' first," muttered the Duke.

Despite lacking social graces, Bridget proved herself once again to be an ace navigator, and soon the minibus was threading its way south along busy roads filled with cars, and queues of double decker buses.

"Giant, red omnibuses," said the Duke. "And not a horse in sight."

"Patience, your Grace, patience. All will soon be revealed," said Parky.

The minibus trundled past Regent's Park, and down the long stretch of Marylebone, heading into the heart of the city. Though the Duke still wasn't saying much, when they drove along the edge of Hyde Park, Stella and Tom could see a light slowly building up in his eyes.

"Merge right," said Bridget, and Parky followed the fast-moving cars ahead of him.

"Bridget, are we going where I think I we're going?" asked the Duke after a time.

"Merge right," said Bridget.

"I do believe we are," said the Duke, coming alive. "I do believe we're heading somewhere very familiar indeed. Parkin, you sly fox!"

Parky steered the minibus around a huge roundabout, in the middle of which was a massive arch with a statue on top. Now the Duke was practically hovering in the back seat. He gestured at a grand building on the far side of the roundabout, protected behind a high, iron fence. "Look, twins, look," Wellington gasped. "Apsley House!" Made of sand-coloured stone, with four enormous columns above its entrance, and archways below, it was a real palace.

"Arriving at destination, on right," said Bridget with a suggestion of laughter.

"Number One, London, residence of the Duke of Wellington,[9]" said Parky, "and from what I know, things haven't changed much."

---

[9] Apsley House really does have the address, Number One, London. And to this day, the descendants of the 1st Duke of Wellington still call it home.

"You really mean it?"

"A friend of mine looks after the place. Now let's find somewhere to put the minibus shall we? Parking is a nightmare around here." Parky eventually found a car park a short walk from Apsley House, and brought the castle minibus to a stop in the last free space.

"I really can't wait to see the old place," chuckled the Duke. "Fire up the monstrosity!" he said pointing at the ghost trap.

"Yes, sir!" said Stella.

Tom switched the trap to capture, and it began to whirr and hum. Wellington shimmered for a moment, and with the wink of an eye, he disappeared.

"Right, let's go and take a look at the old pile, shall we?" said Parky.

"One thing's for certain, we'll have the best guide there is," said Stella.

Further back in the car park, Seymour Stoneyheart sat in his van and watched Parky and the two children get out. The ghost-catcher sniffed deeply and allowed himself another smile (it was getting to be a bit of a habit). He had been right, then. Parky was carrying a ghost trap and Stoneyheart could practically smell the ghost inside it.

And he knew exactly whose ghost it was.

Stoneyheart quickly grabbed another of his traps and got out of his van. The hunt was back on.

CHAPTER TEN

A battle lost

After the noise and commotion of a traffic-locked London, Apsley House was like a sanctuary. Thankfully, there were few visitors on that particular day, and once past the entrance the twins were able to release the Duke from the box. He sprang out of the funnel like a genie from tales of old.

"I think the same rules ought to apply, your Grace," Parky warned. "If you see someone coming you need to get out of sight."

"Of course, of course," murmured Wellington distractedly. "But look, oh just look!" He spread his arms out wide, taking it all in. "It's almost exactly like I left it."

The Duke swept up the stairs past the grand statue of Napoleon (which the twins thought was a little rude, being totally naked) and into a dazzling room. The walls were covered in striped, golden silk, there were curtains the colour of bright sunshine, and a gilt pattern danced across the domed ceiling.

"Wow!" said Stella.

The Duke beamed. "I thought you might like this one. Fit for a princess wouldn't you say?" He bustled about pointing out valuable bits and pieces. The twins and Parky struggled to keep up.

"Give us a moment," said Tom who was looking at a painting of some soldiers.

"But there's so much I want to show you," said the Duke taking him by the hand (or trying to, anyway). "Wait till you see the next room!"

While the twins and Parky were in the hands of their extremely enthusiastic guide, downstairs at reception, the security guard was giving Stoneyheart a curious eye. Odd little character, thought the security guard. Gloomy sort – dressed head to toe in black.

"Funny that," the guard said handing the ghost trap back to Stoneyheart. "That's the second one of those special cameras I've seen today."

"You don't say," said Stoneyheart.

Once he'd collected his ticket, Stoneyheart fished out an electrical meter from his pocket. He'd used the same device the last time he'd hunted down the ghost of the Duke, and quickly adjusted the settings to Wellington's exact signal. The meter crackled and buzzed, the dial going haywire. "Gotcha!" he hissed, snaking his way past the statue of Napoleon (which he thought was actually a little bit rude), and up the stairs.

Nearby, the Duke was busy showing his friends the most important, most impressive part of the house. The twins had never seen such a thing. Rich maroon walls covered in paintings rose up to the ceiling, which towered miles above their heads. The room was longer than a tennis court, the carpet a plush red, the furniture painted gold.

"It's much fancier than the castle by the sea," Tom whistled.

"I used to hold my famous Waterloo Banquets in here. My table could hold eighty-five!" said the Duke.

"What did you have to eat?" asked Stella.

"Mutton and veg," said the Duke, and Stella wrinkled her nose.

"Well I'm going to give my feet a rest, and see this room properly," said Parky plonking himself down on one of the sofas. The twins joined him.

"But you haven't seen the half of it!" implored the Duke.

"Come back for us in a little bit," suggested Parky. "Give you a chance to be alone with the place."

The Duke thought for a moment. "Capital!" he said with a smile, "I'll return before you know it," and he wandered off.

The Duke passed through the wall into the room next door (checking to see it was empty first), running his hands through all his old possessions. These people really do take a lot of care in looking after the old place, he thought as he wandered around. He would have to get Parky to write a thank-you letter.

A few rooms later, Wellington stopped in front of a large painting showing the battle of Waterloo. It was one of his favourites. In the foreground near a blazing cannon was his famous adversary, Napoleon, surrounded by his officers. In the distance on his chestnut horse was himself, the battle almost won.

And in between the two generals, there were countless soldiers dead and alive. Wellington thought for a moment about all the thousands of men who had fallen. *"Next to a battle lost, the greatest misery is a battle gained,*[10]*"* he said aloud to himself.

---

[10] Again, Wellington really did say those words…

"Well, isn't that the truth," came a voice from behind, breaking him from his thoughts. "Hello, ghostie. Remember me?"

Wellington spun round, just long enough to see Stoneyheart leering at him. In his hands was a ghost trap, funnel aimed. The Duke knew what was coming next. "You bounder!" he barked as he began to flicker, and then vanish as if he had been nothing but a puff of steam.

* * *

"Where on earth could he have got to?" asked Stella. They had long since left the Waterloo Gallery and had traced the Duke's footsteps looking for their friend. It had been an hour since he'd gone and it was getting very near to closing time.

"Perhaps he's just looking at a bit of the house we can't get to?" suggested Tom.

"Could be," said Parky.

"But he did say he'd be back in a moment, and it's not like him not to keep his word."

"Maybe he's suddenly got homesick like the other ghosts?" said Tom. He paused. "Maybe he doesn't want to come back. Maybe he's decided he'd rather stay."

Stella shook her head. "Even if he did, he would never leave without saying goodbye. He just wouldn't."

Parky agreed. "Let's split up and take another walk around."

The three of them doubled back and went off into different rooms, calling out Wellington's name as if he were a prized tabby.

A few minutes later, they met back in the golden room, the first room they had visited.

73

They greeted each other with a shake of the head.

"Now, I have to agree with you, sis, something doesn't feel right," said Tom.

"He couldn't have left the building," said Stella. "So where is he?"

"There's a quick way to find out," said Parky, leading them down the stairs to the reception at the front of the building.

"Hello, Parky," said the woman behind the desk, "enjoy the tour?"

"The place looks smashing, Theresa," said Parky. "You'll have to come and visit us at the castle next time you're down that way."

"I'll do that," said Theresa.

Parky leaned over and pointed at the bank of surveillance screens behind the counter. "Are those the new RX-50s?" he gasped.

"They are – the latest."

"We're thinking about getting them for the castle as it happens. Mind if I have a look?" Parky tugged at his earlobe.

"Help yourself," said Theresa, offering her chair to Parky.

Parky sat down in front of the CCTV screens. The twins could see that there were several screens covering the entrance. "This is all very efficient," said Parky. "How do you rewind?"

Theresa leaned over. "You just twiddle that dial there."

Parky found the camera pointed at the front door and quickly wound the footage back. He didn't have to go far. The answer slapped them in the face, in plain black and white. Parky's eyes widened. The man in his long, black coat and wide-brimmed hat. Leaving the building in a hurry, carrying a black box with a funnel at the end. Stoneyheart. Parky would recognise him anywhere. Stella and Tom stood very still.

"Brilliant cameras, aren't they?" said Theresa.

CHAPTER ELEVEN

Another wild ghost chase

Back in the minibus, the three friends were still in a state of disbelief. Stoneyheart! Questions flew around like flies. What was he doing at Apsley House? How had he found them? What were they going to do? There was only one thing they were fairly sure of, that Stoneyheart had ghost-napped the Duke.

"Let's go to the police," suggested Tom.

"I don't think so," said Stella. She mimed putting a phone to her ear, "Hello, police... can you help us? We think our friend the Duke of Wellington, has been ghost-napped. Yes, that's right, the Duke of Wellington... hero of the battle of Waterloo... died in 1852... that's the one," she pretended to hang up.

"Good point," said Tom.

"Yes, I think Stella's right, we need to find our own way to get the Duke back," said Parky.

"Where do you think Stoneyheart takes his ghosts?" asked Tom.

Parky thought for a moment. "He keeps loads stored at home, like trophies in a cabinet. I remember he told me."

"Like a horrible hunter with the heads of all the animals he's killed," Tom grimaced.

"Let's have a look at your phone, then," said Stella. Parky handed it to her. "I bet his business has a website."

"Nuisance Control Services, I think it was," said Parky.

Stella tapped in the name and waited for the search results. She scrolled through lots of rat-catchers and insect-sprayers and silverfish removers, but finally she found it. 'Nuisance Control Services: Guaranteed,' with a photograph of Stoneyheart in a dramatic pose, ghost trap at the ready.

Stella tapped the link for *contact* and it gave an address.

"That's not far from here," said Parky, starting up the engine and setting Bridget.

"In one hundred yards turn right," said Bridget. "Turn right!"

The minibus roared through London, heading south, Bridget giving instructions as if she were taking part in a rally. She had Parky ducking down alleys and whizzing over crossings, changing gears up and down, visiting parts of London he had never seen before.

"The sooner we get there, the better. You never know what that man Stoneyheart has in mind," said Parky.

* * *

With his van safely parked outside his shop, and his front door locked and bolted, Stoneyheart placed the ghost trap on his desk and contemplated his prize catch, rather pleased with himself. Wellington might have been a great military leader when he was alive, but this ghost, this nasty jumble of electromagnetic energy had been outflanked like a novice. It would add that extra-special something to his trophy cabinet.

Stoneyheart opened the door to his vault. It was a dark, windowless room rammed full of boxes with funnels and flashing red lights. A ghost treasury. There were some impressive ghouls trapped on those shelves, thought Stoneyheart. But Wellington's apparition was the biggest prize of all. He carefully chose a worthy spot, and slotted the ghost trap into place. It would never see the light of day again.

* * *

"Now what?" asked Stella.

The twins and Parky parked themselves across the street from Stoneyheart's headquarters. Wedged between a kebab shop and a drain unblocking company, Nuisance Control Services looked a bit like an undertakers. Tom was expecting an evil lair with drawbridges and iron bars, and was a bit disappointed.

"I reckon we stroll in there and tell Stoneyheart to hand him over," he suggested.

"A little lacking in style, wouldn't you say?" said Stella.

"As much as I'd very much like to take the direct route and even punch him on the nose, Tom, it would be better if we could avoid a confrontation," agreed Parky.

"Then how about another wild ghost chase," said Tom. "Send him off for a spin, and while he's out we go in and nab the Duke."

"Now you're talking," said Stella.

"We need a good story… " said Parky, tugging at his earlobe.

Stoneyheart was just settling down to a plate of pilchards on toast when the phone went. With a disgruntled sigh, he let it go through to his answering machine.

"Is this the right number for a ghost-catcher?" The voice coming through on the speaker sounded old and frail "… is anyone there…? Oh dear… it's just that we have a bit of an emergency. I'm one of the Beefeaters. Calling from the Tower of London."

A fish dropped from Stoneyheart's gaping mouth. He scrambled for the phone.

"I'm here, I'm here," he said spraying pilchard onto the receiver. "Sorry to keep you waiting," he listened, his eyes flickering. Tower of London. Beefeater. He quickly did some sums. Ka-ching!

Stoneyheart grabbed a pen and paper and took notes. "Terrible ghost… headless… scared half the tourists away… Anne Boleyn!" Celebrity ghost! Stoneyheart quickly added a nought to the end of his price. "I'll be there right away. Tell the other Beefeaters to stay clear of that foul ghoul. I'm on my way."

In the minibus outside, Stella and Tom creased over in laughter. "Beefeater? Anne Bolyen?[11] A little over the top isn't it?"

"He didn't seem to think so," said Parky, nodding across the road as Stoneyheart burst out of his office and launched himself into his van. With a screech of tyres, the van lurched away.

---

[11] One of Henry VIII's unfortunate wives, and yes, she was beheaded.

"Now that should buy us at least an hour," said Parky.

"With any luck they'll lock him up overnight," said Tom. "Toss him in the dungeon and let the ravens peck at him.[12]"

Parky and the twins quickly crossed the road and cased Stoneyheart's place.

"Look, he's left something unlocked," Stella pointed at a small window in the flat above the shop. "If we could get up there, I bet I could squeeze in through that bathroom window."

Parky chuckled. "She came in through the bathroom window! Get it?" The twins looked at him blankly. "Don't you see? The famous song?" he tried. More blank looks. "What do you two know anyway?" Parky sighed.[13]

"If we're all done with the pop quiz, perhaps we could get me up there," said Stella.

"Well, we could do it your way," said Tom, "or we could just use the front door." Tom gave the door to Stoneyheart's office a push, and it swung wide open.

---

[12] The famous ravens of the Tower of London. It is said that if they ever leave, the tower will fall.

[13] She came in through the bathroom window: by Sir Paul 'Macca' McCartney. I'm humming it as I write…

"He was in such a hurry, he must have left that unlocked too," said Parky.

The three friends stepped inside and quickly locked the door behind them. They passed through the office, which only had an uninteresting desk and some uninteresting chairs, and headed for the door marked 'private.' Inside, there were some stairs to the flat above, and another door. Cautiously, Parky pushed it open.

It was the ghost vault. If the outside of Stoneyheart's shop had been boringly plain, the vault did not disappoint. Shelves ran the length of the room, reaching from the floor right up to the high ceiling – you needed a ladder to get to the very top. And packed onto the shelves like books in a library were ghost traps. Too many to count. A bank of funnels and flashing lights. The room practically throbbed in the gloom.

"Wow," said Tom staring up at the shelves. "And to think each one of those traps has a spirit inside it."

"There must be hundreds of them. How are we supposed to know which one is the Duke?" Stella asked. She had a point. Each trap had a label on it with a number written in tidy writing, but the numbers seemed quite random and there were no names.

Parky ran his hand down one of the shelves. "Do any of them look more recent than the others? Any of them less dusty?" The three of them started looking, but couldn't spot the odd one out. All the ghost traps were immaculate.

"Maybe Stoneyheart keeps a list somewhere," said Stella. Again, a quick search revealed nothing.

"Well, there's only one option," said Parky.

"Keep turning the traps to release until the Duke pops out," said Tom.

"Fun!" said Stella.

CHAPTER TWELVE

Duncan MacAngus, poet

Tom hurried down one row of boxes, flicking each one to 'release', and clouds of steam flowed into the room. The three friends stepped back. You never knew just who you might run into.

The first person to emerge from the steam was a doctor in a white coat armed with a clipboard. She looked around at the vault briefly, but didn't seem put out in the slightest that she appeared to be in some kind of storage room. She quickly advanced on Parky. "Aha! Now what seems to be the problem?"

"Nothing," said Parky.

"Tsk, tsk," said the Doctor putting on her stethoscope. "You look quite ill to me."

"If you wait just a moment, I can explain," said Parky, raising his hands. But he was interrupted by

85

the arrival of the second ghost and then the third: a man in an old-fashioned flying helmet and goggles, and a trapeze artist with a pointy moustache and a stripy leotard. They looked the vault up and down, alarmed.

"Have you noticed how all the ghosts we find are really curious characters?" whispered Stella.

"Well, he looks ordinary," said Tom pointing at the fourth ghost to come out of a box. He was a tiny man in a drab suit, with half-moon glasses and a pencil behind his ear.

"Shhhh!" the man said, wagging his finger at Tom. "There will be no talking in the library!"

One by one, the other boxes on the shelf began to open. There was a lollipop lady, a street cleaner, a butcher, a baker and a candlestick maker. Two accountants, one mime artist dressed in black with her face painted white, and a parking warden. Everyone standing shoulder to shoulder and talking loudly. But no Wellington.

"If you'll please come upstairs to the flat," said Parky showing all the ghosts to the stairs. "Make yourselves right at home, and all will be made clear soon enough."

"My turn," said Stella when the room had been cleared. She chose a shelf and hit release on every box.

The second shelf revealed eleven cricketers dressed in whites and a supermarket checkout boy. They too drifted up the stairs and into Stoneyheart's flat.

"Better luck next time," said Tom.

Parky checked his watch, "We need to get a move on. Stoneyheart has probably worked out he's been tricked by now. If he finds us here and calls the police, we'll really be in for it." He chose a shelf and started attacking switches.

The first ghost from Parky's shelf to escape wore an enormous kilt and a sporran. He had a beard that tumbled down over his chest, and eyes that blazed savagely. He carried a folder of papers with hands covered in ink stains. Tom and Stella shrunk back.

The man eyed Parky suspiciously, and then the twins, beard twitching. "You didnae happen to see a wee man did ye? Aboot this high?" he held his hand to his waist. "Dressed all in black?"

"You mean Stoneyheart," said Tom, swallowing hard. "The man who trapped you in the box."

"Aye, that's the beastie!"

"We've given him the run around," said Parky, "and now we're freeing all of you." Parky pointed at the rows of boxes. He quickly made introductions.

"The name's Harry Parkin and this is Stella and Tom."

Just then, several more ghosts burst through the mist. They took one look at the fierce Scotsman and shuffled back.

"Nice tei meit all a ye," said the Scotsman addressing the room. "Duncan MacAngus, poet." He tried to shake Parky's hand. "The rogue's oot you say? Then I'll just wait till he gets back. Me and him'll be having a wee dance!" He snorted and growled.

Parky guided the other ghosts up the stairs, but it was clear Mr MacAngus wasn't going anywhere.

"Oh, where are you?" Stella said gazing up at the rows of blinking lights. For the first time, it crossed her mind that they might not find Wellington before Stoneyheart got back. And then what?

"Have ye lost somebody is it?" inquired MacAngus.

Tom nodded. "Our friend. He's here somewhere – along with all the others stolen by Stoneyheart."

"The thieving magpie!" growled MacAngus. He peered up at the shelves. He twitched his beard a little, deep in thought, then he went up to the nearest box and started counting:

"One for sorrow, two for joy,
Three for a girl, four for a boy.
Five for silver, six for gold,
And seven for a secret that must never be told,[14]"

MacAngus pointed to the seventh box. "Try that one, laddie."

Tom couldn't see any chance at all that MacAngus's rhyme would do the trick, but tried it all the same.

Another puff of steam filled the room with a loud hiss, followed by silence. Then came a thunderous voice through the mist, a voice that they all recognised. "By God sir, you'll answer for this!" From out of the mist marched the Duke of Wellington, crackling with rage, his fists raised. He stopped, and immediately broke into a smile. "Oh, it's you! What took you so long?" He threw his arms out wide.

"But how did you know?" Stella asked MacAngus.

---

[14] A traditional rhyme to work out if you'll have good or bad luck. Often said when you're counting magpies…

89

"Dinnae take too lightly the gift of a poem." MacAngus turned to Wellington, "Noo what's the plan?"

"Reverse slope defence," said Wellington. "It worked before, and I think it will do quite nicely now."

CHAPTER THIRTEEN

Waterloo

Stoneyheart scanned his office from across the street, jaw clenched, hat jammed down tighter than normal over his head. The call to the Tower turned out to be a prank of the worst kind. He'd never been so embarrassed in all his life. The Beefeaters had practically rolled around the floor laughing, and even the ravens had cackled.

Stoneyheart smelled a rat. Coming so soon after his visit to Apsley house, this was all something to do with that Wellington ghost, he could feel it. But at the moment, everything seemed fine across the road. There was no movement from the office or from his rooms above. And if Parky and those annoying children had somehow got in, then they'd better be ready for one enormous surprise.

Stoneyheart crossed the road and quietly opened his office door with his key, slipping inside.

Stella popped out from behind a parked car. She turned on a torch and waved it at the flat above.

Inside the office, it was empty. Stoneyheart could see no sign of anyone having been there. He tiptoed through the office and into the hallway. Again, all was as it should be. He pushed open the door to the vault.

Empty.

All the ghost traps were still plugged in. Even his latest acquisition was still where he last put it. Nothing out of place.

Maybe he was jumping to conclusions after all. Stoneyheart took off his hat and coat, hanging them up. Perhaps now he could finish his fish tea. It was then that he heard a noise. It was coming from the top of the stairs: a creaking of a floorboard. Stoneyheart switched on the stairs light. And there on the landing – the boy, one of the children he had seen with Parky. But now he was all on his own, trying his best to creep away, the little guttersnipe.

"Thief!" Stoneyheart shrieked. "Stay where you are!"

Tom froze. "Oops." He took one look at Stoneyheart and then he raced along the landing and up the second flight of stairs.

"Stop!" Stoneyheart bellowed, as he gave chase. He clattered up the stairs and stopped at the top. The boy carried on and disappeared into the flat above, but there was no sign of anyone else. Stoneyheart listened for sounds, checking to see that there was no one else around. That it wasn't a trap like the time at the castle. He strode up the stairs, taking them two at a time. He ran into the flat. Again, it was empty. Not a soul.

"Where are you? Little rat?" Nothing. Stoneyheart heard a sniffle coming from the bedroom down the hallway. He smiled to himself. "Gotcha!" he murmured. "The police are going to lock you up once I press charges."

He was halfway down the hall when the bedroom door swung open. The door to the bathroom on his left swung open too. And then the door to the kitchen on his right: all at once, like three sides of a trap.

"Well, well, well, look what the Tom dragged in," said Wellington, stepping out of the bedroom, with Parky and a squad of ghosts behind him.

"Time to take your *medicine*," said the doctor climbing out of the bathtub.

"Looks a bit of a *sticky wicket*," said a cricketer coming from the kitchen. "Come on, chaps," he called to his team.

Stoneyheart groaned. He inched backwards away from the advancing troops, his head spinning. This wasn't happening. Not again. "Now just hold on a second," he began. The ghosts got closer and Stoneyheart turned to run, to escape back down the stairs. But of course, the way was blocked.

"This is long *overdue*," said the librarian at the front of a ghostly cohort, glaring at Stoneyheart over his spectacles. The ghosts moved in.

Stoneyheart looked this way and that, frantically trying to see a way out.

"There isn't one," said Wellington, reading his mind. "I'm afraid, once again it looks like you've met your Waterloo, Stoneyheart."

Stoneyheart turned back to the stairs. There was nothing else for it. He'd have to run through the crowd of ghouls and hope none of them possessed him. He swallowed.

But then Stoneyheart saw a sight he hoped he'd never have to see again. It was the hardest, most ferocious ghost in the entire world. The only ghost of whom he'd ever been even remotely scared. It was the dead poet, MacAngus.

"Aye, that's right – it's me, ye terrible beastie!" roared the poet MacAngus, pushing his way

through the other ghosts. "Time to get what's coming to ye!"

* * *

Bridget had her instructions. "At the roundabout, take the second exit," she announced.

"How sweet it is to hear your voice, old girl," said Wellington wedged in-between Stella and Tom

95

in the front seat of the castle minibus. His shape flickered happily in the last of the day's light.

"I don't know about you, but I've had enough excitement for one day," said Parky. "I'll be glad to get back to the castle by the sea, that's for sure."

But it was safe to say the three friends weren't taking the shortest route back to the castle. In the back of the minibus were dozens of ghosts, all crammed in, all chattering happily. They too were going home. And back at Stoneyheart's flat there were dozens more having the most amazing party ever. The twins and Parky would come back for them later.

"You have to agree, that was the best wild ghost trip," said Tom.

"Agreed," murmured Wellington. "Top marks."

"We could do it every holiday," said Stella.

"I wonder how MacAngus is getting on," said Parky.

* * *

At Euston railway station a short man, wearing a black hat and black overcoat was at the ticket office of the overnight Scotland sleeper service.

"So it's a single berth, first class, on the train that's just about to depart, one way to Edinburgh?" asked the woman behind the counter.

"Aye, that's right."

"Sure you don't want a return? It's cheaper that way," the woman in the ticket office pointed out.

The man shook his head and pulled out some notes from his wallet. "Nay, something tells me I'll be staying a wee, wee while," he grinned.

Author's Note

Though I've drawn on many real places, and taken inspiration for my character of the ghost of the Duke of Wellington from the historical figure, this is entirely a light-hearted work of fiction, as are all the characters in it. I do hope, however, that reading this book might make you want to visit some of the places that inspired me, and which I used as a basis for the settings. English Heritage do a magnificent job of keeping history alive, and I like nothing better than treading in the paths of the past and picturing all that might have gone on before. Pester your parents.

I owe many thanks: to Jenny, Mia, David and Miles. My dearest and most trusted critics. To my editors, Hannah Rolls and Emily Lunn at Bloomsbury for their careful eyes, and whose suggestions made this a much better read. To Kate Paice for seeing the potential in my books in the first place, and for giving this sequel the green light. And to Mike Phillips whose illustrations are the best bit.

Bonus bits!

Guess who?

Each of the descriptions below relates to one of the following characters:

1 Reg Butcher
2 Gelatina
3 Seymour Stoneyheart
4 Harry Parkin
5 MacAngus
6 Duke of Wellington
7 Bridget
8 Marcus Severus Occulus

Match the character to the description by writing the right letter next to the number on a sheet of paper. Check your answers at the end of this section (no peeking!).

A 'a quiet and gentle soul'
B sets off to find the ghost of Anne Boleyn

C had a dining table that could seat 85 people

D a member of a contubernium

E died playing the part of Morgiana in Ali Baba

F a fan of Fusiliers FC

G provided all of the driving directions

H identified the ghost trap in which the Duke of Wellington was trapped

London now and then

As the group are driving round London the Duke becomes increasingly unsure of the place. He has not seen cars, satnavs and double decker buses before (to name but a few things!). In the time when he was alive London was very different...

Here are a few differences between London at the time of the Duke of Wellington and now:

Then...	Now...
• It was the largest city in the world.	• Tokyo is now the largest (by population).
• By 1815 1.4 million people lived there.	• Over 8.3 million people live in London now.
• Horses and carts were used for transport.	• Now we have cars, buses, motorbikes and more...

More about the Duke of Wellington

There are lots of brilliant history books about the Duke of Wellington, but to whet your appetite, here are a few interesting facts about him:

- He was Irish.
- His name was Arthur Wellesley.
- He became a politician when he was only 20 years old.
- He has at least 90 pubs named after him.
- He was Prime Minister twice.
- He went to Eton school.
- He had two children named Arthur and Charles.
- He was buried in St Paul's Cathedral.

Get out and explore!

There are lots of places mentioned in this book (some are made-up but others are real). Why not suggest to your family that you visit one or more of these places to enjoy history first hand? You can also explore theses places online; their websites have loads of information and sometimes 360 degree visual tours.

Richborough Roman Fort – this fort is in East Kent. It is one of the most important Roman sites in the whole of Britain as it saw both the beginning and end of Roman rule. You could even choose to arrive by boat like the Romans would have done. Keep your eyes peeled for Marcus Severus Occulus and his friends whilst you are there!

Walmer Castle – this is a Tudor castle, also in East Kent and is where the Duke of Wellington died. Here you can see the original wellington boots. Keep your eyes open for any friendly ghosts when you visit!

Apsley House – this is where the Duke of Wellington lived. It is also known as Number 1, London! It is in central London and has mostly been left how it would have been when the Duke lived there. Go and see for yourself but keep an eye out for Seymour Stoneyheart in case he is on ghost-napping duties!

St Paul's Cathedral – this is where the Duke of Wellington is buried and is in central London. Horatio Nelson (another great British military figure) is also buried here, along with many other important people.

What next?

If you enjoyed reading this story and haven't already read the first one, *The Twins, the Ghost and the Castle,* find it, snuggle up somewhere and get reading!

Then, why not have a go at writing your own story about a historical figure that has come back as a ghost? Think about where they might have haunted and write a chapter that could be added to this book.

Answers to 'Guess who':

1F, 2E, 3B, 4A, 5H, 6C, 7G, 8D

The Twins the Ghost and the Castle

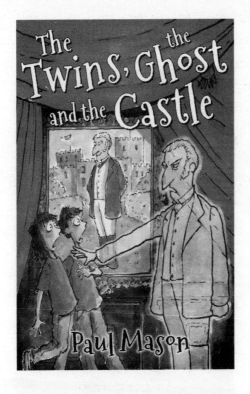

When the twins, Stella and Tom secretly move into a castle they think their problems are over but they are dead wrong. For a start the castle is haunted. And soon a destructive developer and a mean-spirited ghost hunter threatening their happy home.

Can the twins help the ghost and save the castle?

Franklin's Emporium

Coming soon!

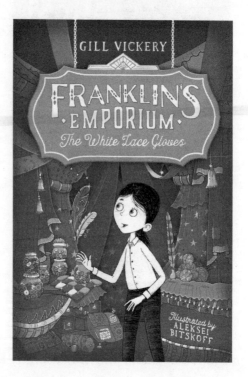

When Alex goes to Golden Bay for the summer wants be left in peace to read her books but her cousin Maisie has other ideas. Soon, Alex ends up in Franklin's Emporium, the department store where there's magic on every floor!